PALACE OF LOST TRIBES: HARRY FISCHER'S DOCUMENTARY

STORY OF PURE SILENCE.

ROHAN KARTIKEYA VELICHERLA

Made with ♥ on the Notion Press Platform
www.notionpress.com

I dedicate this book to all horror enthusiasts.

Contents

Preface

Main Character: Harry Fischer

Character Profile:

Age: 23

Background: A fresh but talented documentary researcher, eager to prove himself in the field. Former history student, fascinated by lost civilizations.

Personality: Intelligent, curious, and ambitious but inexperienced. He respects history but doesn't believe in supernatural forces—until the palace proves him wrong.

Motivation: Harry was brought onto the team as an assistant researcher, but he sees this as his chance to break out of the shadows and make a name for himself.

Flaw: His desire to impress Dr. Elias Voss makes him ignore early warning signs. He rationalizes the strange occurrences in the palace—until he can't anymore.

Arc: What starts as a thrilling adventure quickly turns into a nightmare. The whispers begin calling his name specifically, and as the crew disappears one by one, Harry realizes he was meant to be here. The palace has been waiting for him.

Dr. Elias Voss - Character Profile:

The head of the documentary is Dr. Elias Voss, a seasoned but controversial historian and filmmaker obsessed with lost civilizations. Known for his daring expeditions into forbidden places, Elias has built a reputation for uncovering truths that others fear to explore.

Age: 48

Background: Former professor of archaeology, expelled from college for his radical theories about ancient cultures and supernatural rituals.

Personality: Charismatic, intelligent, but reckless. He believes that every myth has a seed of truth and is willing to push boundaries to find it.

Motivation: Elias has spent decades searching for the truth behind the Whispering Palace. He believes the lost tribe may have discovered an ancient, forbidden power—something beyond human comprehension. This documentary is his chance to prove it to the world.

Flaw: His obsession blinds him to danger, and he ignores warning signs that others take seriously. He insists on venturing deeper, even when the crew begins to disappear.

As the horrors of the palace unfold, Elias must face a chilling realization: he might not be the one making the documentary—he might be part of its story.

Crew

The Documentary Crew:

Jonah Price – The cinematographer. Skilled at capturing eerie visuals but deeply superstitious. He is the first to notice strange occurrences.

Samira "Sam" Patel – The sound engineer. She starts picking up whispers and voices on her recordings long before anyone hears them.

Luis Ortega – The survival expert. Hired to keep the team safe, but he's the first to realize that something is stalking them in the ruins.

Daniel Kim – The producer. More concerned with funding and the documentary's success than the team's safety, leading to reckless decisions.

Rebecca Voss – Elias' estranged daughter and assistant. She joined to reconnect with her father but begins to suspect he knows more about the palace than he admits.

Villagers

Mahesh, A well learned Man of his time.

Prologue

Long before history was written, deep in the heart of a forgotten jungle, there stood a palace ruled by a cruel and ancient tribe. They believed in a single, terrifying law—silence was power. No one was allowed to speak, for sound was said to awaken the spirits buried beneath the palace. The few who broke this rule were never seen again, their voices stolen by the darkness itself.

One night, the entire tribe vanished without a trace, leaving the palace abandoned for thousands of years. The jungle swallowed it whole, and soon, it became nothing more than a legend—a place where the wind carried whispers of the lost souls.

Now, a group of researchers has discovered the ruins and sets out to explore them. But as they step inside, the air grows heavy, the silence unnatural. When one of them speaks, the echoes twist into words that were never spoken. Shadows move without light, and unseen hands press against their throats. One by one, they realize they are not alone.

Something still lingers in the palace, something that has been waiting for voices to feed on. The deeper they go, the louder the whispers become—until silence is no longer an option.

The last survivor must uncover the truth behind the tribe's fate before they, too, become just another whisper in the dark. But what if the only way to escape... is to scream?

CHAPTER ONE

The Whispering Ruins

Harry Fischer adjusted the straps of his backpack, his breath coming in short, measured exhales as the jungle mist clung to his skin. The dense canopy above filtered the sunlight into a dim, eerie glow, casting shifting shadows that seemed to move independently. Each step into the overgrown path sent a dull squelch beneath his boots. His camera gear, slung over his shoulder, felt heavier than usual as if the air was pressing down on him.

Dr. Elias Voss led the group, his sharp eyes scanning ahead, fingers trailing over the moss-covered stone markers littering the path. He paused before one, brushing away the damp vegetation to reveal strange, faded symbols. His voice was barely above a whisper.

"The Vashara left these as warnings. We should pay attention."

Warnings.

Harry felt a shiver crawl up his spine but shook it off. He was here to document history, not get caught up in superstitions. Still, the jungle was too quiet. There were no birds or insects, just the sound of their own breathing.

Jonah Price, the cinematographer, let out a forced chuckle. "So what, the ancient tribe put up 'No Trespassing' signs?"

Elias turned, his expression unreadable. "Something like that."

The crew pushed forward, hacking through thick vines, and stepping over twisted roots. And then—

They saw it.

The Whispering Palace.

The ruins loomed before them, its towering stone walls darkened by centuries of rain and decay. Massive archways stretched into the sky, their edges crumbling yet still defiant against time. Vines snaked along the structure, creeping into the cracks, as though the jungle itself was trying to reclaim what had been left behind.

Figures were carved into the walls—hollow eyes, silent mouths. Their expressions were frozen in something that wasn't quite fear, but something worse: knowing.

The air was wrong here. Too still. Too thick.

"Holy shit," Sam Patel, the sound engineer, whispered, tugging her headphones off. Her voice was tight, uneasy. "Do you hear that?"

Harry strained his ears. Silence.

"Hear what?"

Sam frowned, adjusting her audio levels. "That's just it. There's nothing. No wind. No movement. It's like—" she hesitated, her fingers tightening on her recorder. "Like the jungle doesn't want to get too close."

Rebecca Voss, Elias's daughter and assistant, hugged her notepad to her chest. "Maybe it's just... the acoustics?" But her voice wavered. She didn't believe that. None of them did.

Elias stepped forward, eyes gleaming. "This is it. The heart of the Vashara civilization. And tonight, we uncover its secrets."

Harry hesitated before lifting his camera and pressing the record. The lens focused on Elias silhouetted against the ancient ruins.

Just another documentary. Just another story waiting to be told.

Then—from deep within the palace—a whisper.

A voice. Soft. Breathless.

Calling his name.

Harry whirled around, the camera shaking in his grip. The jungle stretched behind him, empty. The others were still setting up their gear, oblivious.

His heart pounded. Maybe it was just the wind, twisting through the ruins—

The screen of his camera flickered.

And died.

CHAPTER TWO

The Vanishing Echo

Harry cursed under his breath, tapping the side of his camera. The screen remained black. He flipped the battery compartment open and checked the charge—full. There was no reason it should have shut off.

"Problems already?" Jonah asked, setting up his tripod nearby.

"Yeah, my camera just...died," Harry muttered, shaking it slightly. "It was fine a second ago."

Elias, already halfway up the cracked stone steps leading into the palace, turned back. "Electronic failures aren't uncommon in places like this. The humidity, the age of the structure—it all interferes. Just keep trying."

Harry wasn't convinced. But before he could say more, Sam made a sound low in her throat.

"Guys," she said, her voice tight. "I'm picking up... something."

Luis Ortega, the survival expert, walked over. "Something?"

Sam adjusted the dials on her sound recorder, pressing the headphones tighter against her ears. "It's faint, but...it almost sounds like—" She paused, swallowing hard. "Whispering."

Harry felt a chill crawl up his arms. "Like us?"

Sam hesitated. "No. Not like us."

Rebecca stepped closer, her fingers digging into her notebook. "Maybe we're picking up interference from the wind?"

"There is no wind," Luis pointed out.

The group stood silent for a moment, as if testing his words. He was right. The jungle behind them was still. No rustling leaves, no distant animal calls. The only sound was their breathing.

Then, from deep inside the palace, a door slammed shut.

Everyone jumped.

"What the hell was that?" Jonah hissed, grabbing his camera.

Elias didn't flinch. Instead, he smiled. "Looks like we aren't alone."

Rebecca's voice was barely above a whisper. "I don't think that's a good thing."

Elias started forward. "We came here to find the truth. Let's not be afraid of it now."

Harry exchanged a glance with Sam, who looked just as uneasy as he felt. But they had come too far to turn back now. Swallowing his fear, he reset his camera and stepped into the darkness of the palace.

As the last of them entered, the jungle outside seemed to exhale.

And the whispers... grew louder.

CHAPTER THREE

Shadows in the Halls

The air inside the palace was thick, damp, and heavy with the scent of decay. Dust floated in the beams of their flashlights, casting eerie patterns on the stone walls. The deeper they ventured, the more the carvings changed—figures twisting, their hollow eyes seeming to follow the crew's every movement.

"Alright," Elias said, his voice barely above a whisper. "Let's split up and document everything we can."

"Split up?" Rebecca's voice was sharp with concern. "Is that really a good idea?"

Elias gave her a calm look. "We cover more ground that way."

No one argued, but an uneasy silence settled over them. Jonah and Luis moved toward the eastern corridor, while Elias, Rebecca, and Sam headed left. That left Harry alone, tasked with filming the central chamber.

As he set up his camera, he noticed something odd. The carvings... had changed. He was sure they had been still before, but now, the figures' mouths were open.

A breath of cold air brushed against his neck.

Then—

A whisper.

"Harry."

The voice came from behind him.

Spinning around, his flashlight beam cut through the darkness. Nothing.

His heart pounded. He had imagined it. He had to have imagined it.

Then, his camera screen flickered.

And the figures... moved.

A scream tore through the palace.

Harry whipped around, recognizing the voice—Rebecca.

He bolted down the hallway, his flashlight beam bouncing wildly off the walls. The air seemed thicker now, pressing against him, slowing him down. The whispers grew louder, layered voices speaking in a language he couldn't understand.

He skidded to a stop as the others converged in a wide, darkened chamber.

Rebecca was on the floor, her eyes wide with terror. "Something—someone—grabbed me."

Luis helped her up, scanning the room. "There's no one here."

Sam turned, her voice trembling. "Then who shut the door?"

Behind them, the entrance to the chamber had sealed.

And from the darkness beyond, the whispers... began to laugh.

Horrifying...

CHAPTER FOUR

The Endless Night

The crew had no choice but to push forward. The deeper they ventured, the more distorted the architecture became. Corridors looped in ways that didn't make sense. Doors led to places they had already been. The palace was shifting around them, trapping them in a labyrinth of darkness and whispers.

Harry clutched his camera tightly, the weight of it suddenly reassuring. It was the only thing tethering him to reality as the air grew thick, the shadows stretching unnaturally. His breath came in shallow gasps. Something was watching them. He could feel it.

"We should stick together," Sam whispered. "I don't like this."

Elias, however, remained unfazed. "Keep documenting everything. This is history—"

A low moan rumbled through the halls, silencing him.

It didn't sound human.

Jonah swung his flashlight toward the far end of the corridor. A figure—tall, skeletal, and impossibly still—stood in the doorway. Its hollow eyes gleamed in the dim light. It didn't move, but Harry swore he could hear it breathing.

Then, the lights flickered.

The figure vanished.

Rebecca let out a choked sob. "We need to go. Now."

Elias hesitated. "We need—"

A shriek split the air. Sam was yanked backward into the shadows, her scream echoing before it abruptly cut off. Harry lunged forward, his fingers grazing the sleeve of her jacket before she was gone.

"No!" Harry shouted, spinning around. "Sam! Where are you?"

The whispers grew louder. The palace was laughing.

Luis grabbed his shoulder. "We have to move! Now!"

Elias led them forward, but every turn only led to more darkness. More corridors. More doors. They were running in circles. The palace wasn't letting them leave.

Jonah fumbled with his radio. "Sam! If you can hear us, say something!"

Static.

Then—

A distorted voice. "Help... me..."

Rebecca clapped her hands over her mouth, tears spilling down her cheeks. "Oh my God."

Harry's hands shook as he lifted his camera. The viewfinder flickered to life, revealing something none of them could see.

Sam. Standing at the end of the hallway.

Except... it wasn't her.

Her body was rigid, her head tilted at an unnatural angle. Her mouth was open too wide, her eyes nothing but black voids. And behind her—the figure loomed.

Harry dropped the camera. "RUN!"

The crew bolted, their frantic footsteps slamming against the ancient stone floor. The palace twisted around them, warping, pulling them deeper. The whispers turned into howls. Shadows stretched, reached—

Then, Luis screamed.

Harry turned just in time to see hands dragging him into the floor. The stone had liquified beneath him, swallowing him whole. He clawed at the surface, his fingers scraping against the slick, blackened rock. His screams turned to gurgles—

And then he was gone.

Rebecca collapsed, sobbing. Jonah backed against the wall, his breathing ragged. "We're gonna die here."

"No," Elias said, his voice eerily calm. "We finish what we started."

Harry stared at him in disbelief. "Are you insane? People are dying!"

Elias's eyes gleamed in the darkness. "And we're closer than ever to understanding why."

Something moved in the corner of Harry's vision. He turned too late.

The last thing he saw was a pair of hollow, grinning eyes.

CHAPTER FIVE

The Silent Call

The air was suffocating. It pressed against Harry's chest, thick with the scent of damp stone and something metallic—blood. His heartbeat pounded in his ears as he stumbled forward, dragging Rebecca with him. Jonah was ahead, his flashlight barely cutting through the darkness that felt alive, shifting, curling, whispering.

"As if someone's gonna kill us in cold blood," Jonah muttered. His voice was flat, almost defeated. "Don't worry, Harry. We'll be okay."

But he didn't sound convinced.

Behind them, something moved.

The whispers slithered along the walls, crawling under their skin. The palace wasn't just shifting—it was breathing. The very walls seemed to inhale and exhale, ancient stones grinding together like teeth. The carvings they had passed earlier—hollow-eyed figures frozen in silent screams—were different now.

They were watching.

Rebecca clutched Harry's sleeve. "I don't think we can get out," she whispered. Her breath was hot against his arm, but she was trembling. "It won't let us."

Jonah stopped so suddenly that Harry nearly crashed into him. "Elias is gone."

"What?"

Harry whipped his flashlight around. He was right. Elias, who had been leading them moments ago, was no longer there. The path behind them stretched into complete darkness. No footprints. No sign of struggle. Just gone.

Rebecca let out a shaky breath. “This isn’t real. This isn’t real.”

But it was.

A laugh—low, guttural, wrong—echoed down the corridor. It wasn’t Elias. It wasn’t Sam or Luis. It wasn’t human.

Then, the sound of footsteps.

Slow. Deliberate. Hunting them.

Jonah gripped his camera like a weapon. “Keep moving.”

They obeyed, quickening their pace. The hallway stretched endlessly, walls pulsing like veins. Shadows darted at the edges of their vision, moving too fast to be tricks of the light.

Then, the whispers stopped.

Silence.

And in that silence, a voice—

“Harry.”

It was Sam’s voice.

Harry froze. He knew better. He knew Sam was dead.

But the voice was right next to him.

“Harry.”

A cold breath on his ear. Not Sam.

His instincts screamed at him to run. But his body wouldn’t move. Something held him in place. He could feel it—long fingers brushing against his back.

Then—

Jonah grabbed his arm and yanked him forward. “Don’t look. Just run.”

Harry obeyed, forcing his legs to move. They sprinted down the corridor, Rebecca sobbing, Jonah cursing under his breath. The laughter followed them, growing louder, closer, inside their heads.

Then—

A door. Massive. Ancient. Bleeding.

Jonah didn’t hesitate. He threw his weight against it, shoving it open.

They stumbled inside—

And the door slammed shut behind them.

CHAPTER SIX

•••

The room was unlike the others. Grand, cavernous, with torches burning without fire, their blue glow casting ghostly light across the walls. The carvings were everywhere—hundreds of figures, mouths open in silent agony.

And at the center—

A throne.

Carved from black stone, towering, twisted, waiting.

Rebecca clutched Jonah's sleeve. "What is this place?"

Jonah didn't answer. He was staring at something beyond them, his face pale, his hands trembling.

Harry followed his gaze—

And his stomach dropped.

Elias stood before the throne.

But it wasn't Elias anymore.

His skin was stretched too tight, his eyes sunken and black. His mouth twitched at the corners, pulled into something that was almost a smile. His fingers curled over the armrests, nails digging into the stone.

And when he spoke, his voice was layered—Elias's and something else.

"You should not have come."

Rebecca screamed.

The torches flickered.

And the palace came alive.

CHAPTER SEVEN

The Awakening

"No! We need to leave! Right now!" Harry's voice was desperate, his eyes darting between Jonah and Rebecca, but neither of them moved. The room felt tighter, the air pressing down on them, but they just stood there, staring at Elias.

Jonah shook his head. "We can't leave. Not yet."

Rebecca wiped sweat from her forehead, her face blank. "He's still Elias. We can save him."

Harry felt a cold chill run down his spine. They weren't listening. They weren't thinking. It was as if the palace had already taken hold of them.

Elias tilted his head, his sunken eyes gleaming. "Leave?" His voice slithered through the air, layered with something ancient. "There is no leaving."

A deep rumble vibrated through the floor. The walls trembled. The torchlight flickered wildly, casting twisted shadows across the carvings. And then—

The statues lining the walls lit up.

Their hollow eyes glowed with an eerie, pulsating light, as if awakening after centuries of slumber. Their carved mouths stretched open in silent screams, and the flickering flames reflected their agony onto the stone floor.

And then—

The lion.

The massive stone carving in the center of the room. Its eyes burned emerald green, its paw slowly rose, the heavy stone grinding like bone against bone.

Harry grabbed Rebecca's wrist. "MOVE!"

But before they could react, the lion's mouth gaped open, and from its cavernous maw—

A thick green gas erupted.

It hit them like a wave. The moment it reached Harry's nostrils, his vision blurred. His body felt sluggish, heavy. The torches warped into spinning orbs of light, and the walls twisted as if melting. The ground beneath him lurched, and suddenly—

He was falling.

Falling into darkness.

His limbs wouldn't move. The gas filled his lungs, wrapping around his mind like tendrils. The last thing he heard before the world slipped away was Elias's voice—

"Now, you will see."

And then—

Everything went black.

Hallucinations began.

CHAPTER EIGHT

Fractured Reality

Harry stood in the hallway of his old high school. The lockers stretched endlessly in both directions, the fluorescent lights above flickering erratically. His breath hitched. No. This isn't real.

But as he turned, he saw the faces of his old classmates, whispering, staring, judging.

"You failed, Harry," a voice echoed.

He snapped his head toward the sound. His teacher, Mr. Callahan, loomed over him, holding a report card with bold red letters scrawled across the page: FAILED.

“No,” Harry muttered, shaking his head. “This isn't real.”

But it felt real. The weight of the paper in his hands, the disappointment in Mr. Callahan's eyes, the laughter of his classmates—it crashed into him like a wave. No, no, no...

Suddenly, the world shifted.

He was no longer in the hallway. Instead, he found himself sitting at a candlelit table in a cozy restaurant. Across from him, Belle Jones smiled nervously, tucking her blonde hair behind her ear. Harry's stomach twisted.

His first date.

He remembered this moment. He had been so happy.

But then, Belle's expression changed. Her eyes darkened, lips trembling. “Why did you do this to me?” she asked.

Harry's hands clenched the table. “What?”

“You dumped me, Harry.” Her voice was barely a whisper, but it echoed like a scream. The restaurant around them darkened, the candles flickering wildly. Belle's face twisted into something unrecognizable, something hollow. "You hurt me. You hurt everyone."

This isn't real.

But it felt so real.

Before he could speak, the world collapsed.

A dark alley. Cold air. Heavy breathing.

Harry turned—and saw him.

A man in a tattered hoodie, eyes wild with rage. A knife gleamed in his trembling hand. The madman on the run.

Harry knew what was coming. He had read about it in the news. This man had stabbed someone fourteen times.

The man lunged.

Pain exploded in Harry's chest. Once. Twice. Again. And again.

Hot blood soaked his shirt. He gasped, choking on air, his vision fading.

The world around him spun, warping, unraveling—

And then—

He woke up. What did he wake up to? Reality?

CHAPTER NINE

The Abyss Calls

Harry's eyes snapped open. Everyone was gone.

The once-crowded room now stood empty, the eerie silence pressing against his skull. His breath came in short, ragged gasps as he spun around, searching. Jonah? Rebecca? Elias?

Nothing.

His heartbeat thundered in his ears. Was this another hallucination?

"Hello?" His voice barely carried in the vast emptiness. No response. No whispers. No shifting walls. Just nothing.

Then, laughter.

Not normal laughter. Maniacal. Twisted. Overlapping voices.

It came from nowhere and everywhere, drilling into his skull. Harry clutched his head, stumbling backward. "Stop! Stop! STOP!"

His foot slipped. The room shifted.

Darkness swallowed him whole.

When he opened his eyes again, he was somewhere else.

His feet were submerged in cold, stagnant water. The dim glow of torches barely illuminated the vast, cavernous chamber. The air was thick with the stench of decay, the walls slick with moisture.

At the far end of the room, a figure stood.

Tall. Cloaked. Waiting.

Its skeletal fingers curled around a rusted scythe. A hollow void where its face should be.

The Grim Reaper.

"Time's up, Harry Fischer."

Harry couldn't breathe. His body refused to move. The water around his ankles darkened—thick like ink. Like blood.

The floor beneath him vanished.

He plunged downward, spiraling into the abyss.

And then—his past unfolded before him.

Age 8.

Harry stood in his childhood backyard, a wooden stick in his hands. His best friend, Daniel, cowered before him, clutching his arm where Harry had struck him.

"I didn't mean to," Harry whispered, but the image froze, etched into the darkness.

Age 9.

His school desk. A math test. His eyes darting to his classmate's answers. Cheating.

Age 17.

His friend, Liam, staring blankly at the wall, eyes red from crying. "You never listen, Harry. You never cared."

Liam's depression. His isolation. Harry's fault?

Age 19.

A drunken fight. A broken friendship. Words he couldn't take back.

Age 21.

A moment of cowardice. A choice that cost someone dearly. A mistake that never left him.

Age 23.

His biggest mistake.

Coming here.

The abyss screamed.

The weight of his failures crushed him, suffocating, devouring.

And then—

A sharp gasp. His lungs burned. His body jerked awake. But it was not him. Was it?

CHAPTER TEN

The Vanishing

Harry's body trembled as he gasped for air. His eyes adjusted to the dim surroundings, and then—

His heart nearly stopped.

His coworkers lay sprawled across the cold stone floor, their bodies motionless. Rebecca, Jonah, Luis—all of them.

"Wake up! Come on, wake up!" Harry shook Rebecca's shoulder, then Jonah's, but their bodies remained limp. Panic surged through him. He checked for a pulse—they were alive. But no matter how hard he tried, they wouldn't wake.

Then—

A sound.

Footsteps. Slow, deliberate, echoing through the chamber.

Harry's blood turned to ice.

Someone was watching.

A figure loomed in the shadows, hidden just beyond the reach of his flickering flashlight. A whisper—low and unintelligible—curled through the darkness. The air thickened, pressing against his chest like a suffocating weight.

Something was there.

Harry clenched his fists, rage boiling inside him. He had reached his limit. The fear, the hallucinations, the never-ending torment—he had enough.

"WHO.. WHOS THERE!?" he screamed into the void. His voice cracked, raw with frustration and terror.

Silence.

"Dr.Elias? Is that you? ELIAS??"

The footsteps stopped.

Whoever—whatever—was lurking in the darkness had frozen, as if Harry's outburst had startled it.

He didn't wait to find out. Gritting his teeth, he hoisted Rebecca over his shoulder and dragged Jonah by the arm. One by one, he pulled them toward the corridor, his body aching with every step. He had to get them out.

The hallway seemed longer than before, twisting unnaturally as if the palace itself was resisting him. The walls groaned, the flickering torchlight distorting shadows into writhing shapes.

Finally—

The exit.

Harry stumbled outside, collapsing onto the damp grass. The cold air burned his lungs, but he didn't care—they were out.

But then, his stomach dropped.

Elias was missing.

A sharp pain lanced through his skull. And suddenly, memories flooded back—all the colleagues who had gone missing.

The expedition had started with more people.

Where were they now?

CHAPTER ELEVEN

The Missing Ones

Harry sat on the damp ground, his fingers trembling as he took in the horrific realization.

Elias was gone.

But he wasn't the only one.

He ran a mental count. Seven. There were seven others in the crew. The camera team. The historians. The intern they barely spoke to. Gone.

Their names flooded his mind—

Jonah Price – The cinematographer. Skilled at capturing eerie visuals but deeply superstitious. He was the first to notice strange occurrences.

Samir "Sam" Greaves – The sound engineer. He started picking up whispers and voices on his recordings long before anyone heard them.

Luis Ortega – The survival expert. Hired to keep the team safe, but he was the first to realize that something was stalking them in the ruins.

Daniel Kim – The producer. More concerned with funding and the documentary's success than the team's safety, leading to reckless decisions.

Rebecca Voss – Elias' estranged daughter and assistant. She joined to reconnect with her father but began to suspect he knew more about the palace than he admitted.

A rustling in the distance.

Then, the low rumble of approaching engines.

Headlights sliced through the early morning mist, and soon, a convoy of jeeps emerged from the trees. The local guides had come back to pick them up.

One of them—a burly man in a worn-out cowboy hat—stepped out and frowned. His thick Southern drawl cut through the silence.

"Where y'all friends?" he asked, glancing around. "Don't see 'em."

Harry couldn't answer. His throat tightened. They were gone.

Jonah and Rebecca stirred beside him, groggy but alive. Samir sat up, rubbing his temples, while Luis and Daniel groaned in confusion. But the others—

They had vanished.

"Son," the guide pressed, concern flickering across his rugged face, "where the hell is the rest of yer crew?"

Harry shook his head, tears stinging his eyes. What had he agreed to? What had he failed to do?

He scrambled for his backpack, yanking out the hard drive that stored their footage. He fumbled with the camera, desperate to see something—anything.

But as he played the footage—

Nothing.

The files were corrupted.

The last recording that remained showed only static.

And then, just before the screen went black—

A single frame.

A silhouette standing in the palace halls, staring at the camera.

Watching.

The realization struck him like a hammer to the chest. Whatever had taken them—it was still watching.

And now, it knew who was left.

CHAPTER TWELVE

Into the Unknown

Harry couldn't rest. The moment they left the palace grounds, an unbearable weight settled on his chest. Elias, David, Miriam, Sam, Angela, Omar, Benji—they were still out there. Somewhere.

The jeeps rumbled along the dirt road, kicking up dust as they moved farther from the ruins. The other survivors were silent, their faces pale, eyes distant. But Harry couldn't just leave. He needed answers.

"We have to go back," he finally said, his voice firm.

Luis scoffed. "Go back? Are you out of your mind?"

Rebecca, clutching her father's notebook, looked up. "Harry's right. My dad wouldn't just disappear. He knew something. Maybe it's in his notes."

Luis, usually the level-headed one, exhaled sharply. "We barely made it out alive. What if we go back and don't make it out next time?"

Harry shook his head. "We don't have a choice. They're still out there. We owe it to them."

Jonah rubbed his face, looking exhausted. "Then we need a plan. We can't just walk back in blind."

Sam, still shaken, checked his recording equipment. "I've got some strange audio from the last night. Maybe there's a clue in it."

The guide driving the jeep gave them a long look. "Y'all crazy. That place ain't meant for the livin'."

Harry ignored him. His mind was already set. He was going back.

The night air grew colder. The deeper they traveled into the wilderness, the stronger the feeling in Harry's gut became—

The palace wasn't done with them yet.

CHAPTER THIRTEEN

The Lost Recording

As the jeeps pulled into a nearby village, Harry grabbed Sam's recorder. "Play it," he said, his voice urgent.

Sam hesitated but finally pressed play. The static crackled, then the faint sound of footsteps echoed through the speakers. Then a whisper—low, almost too quiet to hear.

"...run...."

Everyone froze.

The voice was familiar. Elias.

Sam adjusted the volume. More whispers followed, overlapping, voices too distorted to understand. Then, a sound that sent chills through the group—laughter. But not just any laughter. His own.

Rebecca gasped. "That's you, Harry."

"I—I don't remember laughing," he stammered.

Then the recording turned into muffled screaming. A sharp static whine burst through the speaker, and the file cut off.

Sam's hands were shaking. "That wasn't there before," he whispered. "I swear."

Luis stood abruptly. "This isn't right. We need to leave."

Before Harry could respond, the village elder approached, his wrinkled face filled with something between fear and pity. "You brought something back with you," he said in a heavy accent.

"What do you mean?" Rebecca asked.

The elder gestured toward the recorder. "The voices. They don't belong here."

Harry exchanged a glance with Sam. "What do we do?"

The elder sighed. “You have two choices: leave now and never return, or go back and make peace with whatever you disturbed.”

Luis scoffed. “Make peace? With ghosts?”

The elder didn’t laugh. “Not ghosts. The ones who were never meant to be found.”

The villagers refused to offer shelter, so the team camped outside the village. That night, Harry couldn’t sleep. Every time he closed his eyes, he saw the palace. The crumbling walls. The eerie statues. The lion’s mouth, pouring out green mist.

And Elias, standing in the darkness, whispering: “Find me.”

Then came the laughter again. His own voice, mocking him.

Harry jolted awake, his breathing ragged. He turned to the others. They were all asleep—except Rebecca. She was staring at the forest, her face pale.

“You hear it too?” Harry whispered.

Rebecca nodded. “We’re being watched.”

From the trees, deep in the shadows, something moved.

They weren’t alone.

The palace wasn’t done with them yet.

CHAPTER FOURTEEN

Divided Loyalties

By morning, Harry and the team sought out the village elders. They needed help—guides, supplies, anything that could aid them in extracting the missing crew. But their request was met with a wall of protest.

The villagers gathered in the central square, voices raised in argument. Some were adamant that the palace was sacred ground, a national landmark that must not be disturbed. Others insisted that it was their duty to help retrieve the lost souls who had wandered into its cursed grasp.

An old man with deep-set eyes raised his voice above the noise. "That place is older than all of us. It has swallowed many before your people came. It will swallow many after."

Harry stepped forward. "We don't want to disturb anything—we just want to find our friends."

A younger villager, clearly torn between fear and duty, spoke. "If we help you, the spirits may never let us return."

Luis folded his arms. "If you don't, we're going in alone."

The crowd muttered. Harry saw uncertainty flicker in some of their faces. Finally, the village elder raised his hand for silence.

"We will give you what we can. But you must promise us one thing—" he paused, looking directly at Harry, "—once you enter that place again, you do not come back."

A heavy silence settled over them.

Harry swallowed hard. He knew they couldn't turn back now.

They had a job to finish.

And a palace full of secrets waiting for them.
The rescue mission was about to begin.

CHAPTER FIFTEEN

Shadows of the Past

Harry took a deep breath. He had made his choice. There was no turning back now.

"We go in, we find them, and we get out," he said, his voice steady. The villagers who had chosen to help stood nearby, their faces hardened with years of fear and superstition. They had finally realized the palace was not just a relic of the past—it was a curse that had tormented them for generations.

As they set off toward the palace, Luis carried extra supplies, Rebecca clutched her father's journal, and Jonah kept his camera rolling. Sam held onto the sound equipment, convinced it might pick up something their eyes couldn't see.

The trek back through the thick jungle was eerily silent. Even the wind seemed to avoid this place.

"We need to examine the footage," Rebecca said, pulling out the camera that had recorded their last moments in the palace.

Jonah rewound the footage to the last few hours before they blacked out. The grainy night vision display flickered, showing the team exploring the main hall. Then came the moment when the lion statue released the gas. Everyone watched as they collapsed, unconscious.

Then something moved in the shadows.

A dark figure lurked just beyond the edge of the frame, barely visible. It was there for a fraction of a second before disappearing behind one of the palace's towering pillars.

"What was that?" Luis whispered, leaning in closer.

Jonah rewound it again. They watched frame by frame.

The shadow shifted.

A hand? A face?

No.

Harry's heart pounded. Had something been watching them the entire time?

Just as the tension reached its peak, rustling sounded in the trees behind them. Everyone spun around, weapons and flashlights at the ready.

Figures emerged from the jungle.

It was the villagers who had opposed them before.

Harry exhaled in relief. "What are you doing here?"

One of the older villagers stepped forward. "We were wrong," he admitted. "For years, we believed the deaths, the bad omens, the disappearances were because of the forest itself. But it was never the forest." He looked at the palace ruins, his face grim. "It was this place. It always has been."

Another villager nodded. "We need to bring it down. We should have done it years ago."

Rebecca clutched her father's journal. "We can't destroy it yet. We still have people inside."

The villagers hesitated, torn between fear and duty.

Harry met their gaze. "Help us find them first. Then you can do what you need to do."

A long silence followed. Then, finally, the village elder nodded. "We move at dawn."

As the moon cast eerie shadows over the ruins, Harry stared up at the looming palace.

This place wasn't just haunted.

It was waiting.

ELIAS was waiting.

CHAPTER SIXTEEN

The Vasharas' Truth

As the first light of dawn cast long shadows over the jungle, the villagers gathered outside the palace ruins, their faces marked with a mixture of fear and grim determination. They had lived under the weight of these ruins for generations, whispering stories of misfortune, of omens that stalked their village like a vengeful spirit. But today, they had chosen to break the cycle. Today, they would uncover the truth.

Harry stood at the forefront, his body aching from the previous ordeal, but his mind sharper than ever. He glanced at Rebecca, who clutched her father's journal tightly, her knuckles white. Jonah adjusted the camera strap across his chest, and Sam stood rigid, as if she could still hear the whispers through her equipment. Luis, ever watchful, surveyed the ruins for any sign of movement.

Among them was Mahesh, a well-learned man among the villagers—one of the few who had studied beyond the borders of his home. Unlike the others, he did not see the palace as a cursed place to be feared but as a mystery to be unraveled. He had spent his life collecting and preserving the stories of their ancestors, and now, standing before the ruins, he felt an overwhelming sense of duty.

"This place was never theirs," Mahesh finally said, his voice firm, yet filled with something akin to sorrow.

Harry turned to him. "What do you mean?"

Mahesh stepped forward, running his hand over the stone pillars. The carvings, though weathered by time, still told a tale—a story long forgotten or perhaps purposefully buried. He wiped away the dust, revealing symbols that did not match those of the Vasharas.

“This palace did not belong to them,” Mahesh continued. “It belonged to a prosperous kingdom—one that thrived long before the Vasharas came. The Vasharas were not the builders. They were invaders.”

The group fell silent. Even the villagers, who had long feared the palace, seemed surprised.

Mahesh moved to another wall, his fingers tracing the faded illustrations. They depicted warriors, not of the Vasharas, but of another civilization—one clothed in ornate garments, standing in peace. Then came the invasion. The murals darkened, shifting to brutal imagery—slaughter, temples burning, the once-holy halls tainted with blood.

Harry clenched his fists. “So they stole this place.”

Mahesh nodded gravely. “Yes. But their conquest came at a price. A guru, a guardian of the palace, cursed them with his dying breath.”

Rebecca flipped through the journal in frantic realization. “My father suspected something about a forced silence... but he never figured out why.”

Mahesh inhaled deeply, his eyes fixated on the next set of carvings. “The guru’s words were simple, but powerful: ‘The one who breaks the silence shall awaken the wrath of the forgotten. The whole tribe will be swallowed by darkness.’”

Jonah shuddered. “The no-talking rule... it wasn’t their way of life.”

“It was their punishment,” Mahesh confirmed. “The Vasharas were forced into silence by fear, terrified that one word would bring forth their doom.”

Luis muttered under his breath, “That’s why they became so ruthless... It wasn’t just greed. It was survival.”

A chill settled over the group. The air in the palace felt heavier now, as if the weight of history pressed upon them. The curse had not just been a legend—it had shaped the very nature of the Vasharas, twisting them from warriors to something far worse.

As they ventured deeper into the ruins, their torches illuminated the remnants of the past—war murals of greed and betrayal, stolen artifacts defiled by time, and bones. So many bones. They lay scattered across the temple halls, some barely recognizable, others eerily preserved.

Yet, there were still no signs of the missing crew.

Harry swallowed hard, his breath shaky. Every step forward felt like walking deeper into something that did not want to be disturbed. They had uncovered the truth of the Vasharas, but that was not why they were here.

CHAPTER SEVENTEEN

Hallucinations... too much

Harry felt a sharp, icy pain rush through his skull as the air around him thickened. His breath hitched. One moment, he was standing amidst the ruins with the villagers and his team. The next, he was drowning in darkness.

Then the visions began.

He was no longer in the palace. He was back in his childhood home, standing in front of a shattered mirror. His reflection was wrong—it twisted and flickered like a broken film reel, flashing different versions of himself. The eight-year-old Harry, clutching a stick, standing over his crying best friend. The thirteen-year-old Harry, gripping a test paper with the answers scribbled in the margins. The seventeen-year-old Harry, turning his back on a desperate friend who needed him. His past mistakes came at him in a vicious cycle, growing darker with each replay.

No. This isn't real. Harry tried to will himself out of the illusion, but the memories wrapped around him like suffocating vines.

Then came the worst of them all.

He was twenty-three again, standing outside the cursed palace, his crew beside him. But something was wrong. He turned to look at them, and his breath caught in his throat.

They were dead.

Jonah lay on the ground, his camera shattered beside him, his throat slit wide open. Sam's face was frozen in horror, her body impaled on a jagged rock. Luis was crumpled in the dirt, eyes staring at nothing. Rebecca's blood-stained hands clutched her father's notebook, her last words forever lost.

Harry stumbled backward, gasping, clutching his head. “No! This isn’t real!”

But the world twisted again. Now, he wasn’t just looking at the dead crew. He was among them.

He could feel it—the weight of the tribe’s garments on his skin, the tightness of the ceremonial mask over his face. The Vasharas were around him, chanting in a language he did not understand, pulling him into their ranks. He was one of them. A silent warrior. A hunter of the cursed palace.

A prisoner of the same fate.

Suddenly, hands gripped his shoulders, shaking him violently. A voice—distant but familiar—was calling his name. He gasped as the darkness shattered like glass, the illusions collapsing into themselves.

His body hit the cold, damp floor of the ruins, his lungs struggling for air.

“Harry! Wake up!”

It was Rebecca. She was alive. So was Jonah. So was Sam. Luis was kneeling beside him, eyes wide with concern.

He wasn’t the only one affected. Jonah had tears in his eyes, muttering something about his own death. Sam held onto Luis, trembling. Rebecca’s breathing was ragged, her hands gripping Harry’s tightly.

Then they heard a sharp inhale. It was Mahesh.

He had collapsed onto his knees, his eyes vacant, as if staring through the walls of time itself. His lips moved soundlessly before he let out a hoarse, trembling whisper.

“I was wrong,” he said, his voice cracking. “I thought we could break the curse.”

His vision had been different, darker. He was no longer in the ruins, but standing in the village. A younger version of himself argued with the elders, his words filled with arrogance and defiance. He had scoffed at their warnings, calling them foolish. He had ventured into the outskirts of the palace years ago, thinking he could prove the legends false. But in his hallucination, he saw the truth—the moment he had unknowingly sealed his own fate.

The spirits of the Vasharas had marked him. Even back then.

Then the vision shifted. The village was burning. Screams filled the air. The same villagers who had stood with him were now twisted shadows, their bodies bound in the same ceremonial garments as the Vasharas. He saw himself among them, but he wasn't just a prisoner—he was leading the rituals. Chanting. Sacrificing. He was one of them.

"Mahesh?" Sam reached for him, and he snapped out of it, choking on his breath. His hands were shaking.

He looked at Harry, horror and guilt reflecting in his eyes. "The palace doesn't just hold the past. It traps the soul. It forces you to see what you fear most."

A cold realization settled over them all.

Rebecca, still holding onto Harry, wiped the tears from her face. Her voice was steady, but her eyes were wide with confusion. "We weren't exposed to the gas, Harry. So why is this happening?"

Mahesh's hands trembled as he finally found his voice. "It's not just the gas. The curse is older than any of us, and it doesn't rely on physical means to affect you. The palace, the Vasharas... they draw you in, make you relive your deepest fears, your worst regrets. The spirits—they don't need to rely on fumes or toxins. The palace itself is a prison of the mind, a place where time bends and the past becomes alive again."

Jonah shook his head, trying to process it. "But if it doesn't rely on the gas... what do we do? How do we escape this?"

Mahesh met his gaze, his eyes hollow. "There's no escaping it. The curse doesn't let go until it has you completely. And each time you think you've broken free... it pulls you back in."

The weight of his words settled like a stone in their stomachs, and the oppressive atmosphere of the ruins seemed to close in around them.

Harry stared into the darkness, the remnants of the hallucinations still echoing in his mind. "So, we're all trapped?"

he muttered, barely able to comprehend it. "How do we fight something we can't even see?"

"By facing it," Mahesh answered softly, his voice heavy with regret. "You have to confront your fears, your past. Only then will you stand a chance of breaking the cycle."

The team exchanged uncertain glances. The path ahead was more uncertain than ever, and the line between reality and illusion was dangerously thin.

CHAPTER EIGHTEEN

The Endless Maze

As the group gathered themselves, their breath ragged and uneven, Mahesh stood up first, his eyes darting around the ruins. The air was thick with tension, but something else seemed to tug at his senses. He stepped forward, scanning the surroundings.

"Wait," he muttered, his voice strained. "This isn't right."

The others turned to look at him, but Mahesh was already moving. His hand brushed against the jagged wall of the ruin, feeling for a hidden passage, a door, or any sign of escape. He stopped abruptly, his face pale.

"It's a maze," he whispered, his voice barely audible.

The others gathered around, confusion painting their faces. "What do you mean a maze?" Sam asked, her tone laced with skepticism.

Mahesh motioned for them to follow him. He led them down a narrow corridor, but when they reached the end, they were met with a blank wall. He turned on his heel and walked in another direction, his brow furrowing in concentration. After a few moments, he came to a stop again, his hand pressed against a smooth stone surface.

"I've been here before," Mahesh said, his voice now shaking with disbelief. "This isn't... this room shouldn't exist. It wasn't here a moment ago."

Luis's eyes widened, his voice low. "You mean the palace is... changing?"

"Exactly," Mahesh replied, turning back to face the group. "It's alive."

The words hung in the air, heavy and unsettling. Rebecca swallowed hard. "What do you mean by that? The palace is alive?"

Mahesh nodded slowly, his mind racing. "This place... it shifts. It's not just a structure made of stone and wood. It reacts to us, to our fears and thoughts. The walls move. The passages change. It adapts. I've heard stories... that the palace can trap souls by making them wander in an endless maze. It twists reality until you can't tell what's real anymore."

Jonah frowned. "That would explain the hallucinations."

"Yes," Mahesh said, his eyes darkened by dread. "And if we're not careful, it will trap us here forever, like it has to so many others before us. This place doesn't want us to leave."

The group exchanged uneasy glances. The thought of the palace itself being sentient, capable of shifting and manipulating its surroundings to torment them, felt far worse than any physical danger they had already faced.

Harry clenched his fists, his jaw tight with frustration. "So how do we get out? How do we stop it?"

Mahesh stared at the walls around them, the maze-like passages stretching endlessly in every direction. "I don't know. But if we're going to survive this, we need to stay together and keep our heads. One wrong turn, and we'll be lost in here forever."

As they stood there, the silence of the palace seemed to hum around them, as though it were waiting for them to make a move—waiting to see who would break first. It felt like the walls were closing in.

The maze had begun, and there was no turning back.

Rebecca's voice was sharp, unwavering, but there was a tremor beneath the surface. Her gaze was fixed, burning with a determination that cut through the tension like a knife.

“We have to find our friends,” she said, her voice low but urgent, “and rescue my dad.” Her hands clenched into fists, and her eyes shone with a mix of desperation and defiance. “We can't leave him like this. Not after everything that's happened."

Harry's heart ached as he saw the storm in Rebecca's eyes. He knew how much her father meant to her. Even though after all the bad things in their realationship. The thought of Elias—once a strong, guiding presence in their lives—now corrupted by whatever dark force had taken hold of him, was unbearable.

He took a step closer, his voice soft but firm. "Rebecca, we will find them. We'll get Elias back. I promise."

Her eyes flickered with uncertainty, but she held his gaze, unwilling to break down. "We don't have time for promises, Harry. We need to move. Every second we waste, they get farther away."

"I know," Harry replied, his voice steady, trying to offer her something that felt like strength. "But right now, we can't let the palace win. It wants to pull us apart, to make us lose our way. But we have to stick together. We need to keep our focus."

Rebecca closed her eyes for a brief moment, her breath shaky as she tried to steady herself. When she opened them again, her expression had hardened. "I can't lose them, Harry. Not like this."

Harry stepped forward and placed a hand gently on her shoulder, his grip firm and reassuring. "You won't lose them. And you won't lose yourself, either. We're not getting trapped in here. We're getting out—together."

For a heartbeat, she let the words settle, her tension easing just slightly under the weight of Harry's calm presence. She took a deep breath, letting the moment of reassurance anchor her, before nodding. "Okay," she whispered, the fire in her eyes reigniting. "We move. Now."

With the group's renewed resolve, they turned and pressed forward through the maze-like corridors, every step echoing in the oppressive silence of the palace. Harry stayed close to Rebecca, sensing the storm still brewing inside her, but seeing the strength in her now, too. They didn't have time to waste. The path ahead was uncertain.

Will they ever find their crew? Or will they too dissappear without a trace.

Stay Tuned

As Harry and the remaining crew struggle to come to terms with what happened in the palace, one question remains: What took the others?

The footage is gone, their memories are fragmented, and the deeper they dig for answers, the more questions arise. Was it the ancient curse? A malevolent force? Or something far worse—something beyond human understanding?

With Elias missing, Rebecca is determined to uncover the truth about her father's past. Harry, haunted by his hallucinations, must decide whether to walk away or venture back into the unknown to find those they lost.

But the palace is not done with them yet.

Something followed them out.

And it's still watching.

What's Next?

This is not the end—only the beginning of a mystery that runs deeper than anyone imagined. Stay tuned for the next book of "Palace of lost Tribes: Harry fischer's Documentary."

Regarding The 3rd Book "when I Was Alone"

Though story is fixed we are thinking of of making the story more magic based and charecter arc based, if you do have suggestions please feel free to write a review!

It will come soon, around christmas of 2026.